To our first grandson —
Yet unseen and unnamed, we await your arrival.
May He who sees you and knows you by name,
be your nearest and dearest treasure—so that all
who see you and know you,
will see Him and love Him.
R.Z.

For Dimitri
L.F.

"Do not store up for yourselves treasures on earth,
where moths and vermin destroy, and where thieves
break in and steal. But store up for yourselves treasures
in heaven, where moths and vermin do not destroy,
and where thieves do not break in and steal.
For where your treasure is, there your heart will be also."

MATTHEW 6:19–21

ZONDERKIDZ

The Merchant and the Thief
Copyright © 2012 by Ravi Zacharias
Illustrations © 2012 by Laure Fournier

Requests for information should be addressed to:

Zondervan, *Grand Rapids, Michigan 49530*

Library of Congress Cataloging-in-Publication Data

Zacharias, Ravi K.
    The merchant and the thief : a folktale from India / by Ravi Zacharias ;
[illustrations by Laure Fournier].
          p.   cm.
    Summary: In this adaptation of an Indian folktale, as a thief travels with a
wealthy jewel merchant he tries and fails several times to uncover and steal his
treasures, but in return the merchant offers the thief God's forgiveness and a
life in Jesus Christ.

    ISBN 978-0-310-71636-5 (hardcover, jacketed printed : alk. paper)
    [1. Robbers and outlaws—Fiction. 2. Christian life—Fiction. 3. India—
Fiction.] I. Fournier, Laure, ill. II. Title.
PZ7.Z167Mg 2012
[E]—dc22
                                                     2010031871

All Scripture quotations, unless otherwise indicated, are taken from the Holy Bible,
New International Version®, NIV®. Copyright © 1973, 1978, 1984, 2011 by Biblica, Inc.™
Used by permission. All rights reserved worldwide.

Any Internet addresses (websites, blogs, etc.) and telephone numbers in this book
are offered as a resource. They are not intended in any way to be or imply an en-
dorsement by Zondervan, nor does Zondervan vouch for the content of these sites
and numbers for the life of this book.

Published in association with the literary agency of Wolgemuth & Associates, Inc.

Zonderkidz is a trademark of Zondervan.

Editor: Barbara Herndon
Cover design: Kris Nelson
Interior design and art direction: Matthew Van Zomeren

Printed in China

11 12 13 14 15 /GPC/ 22 21 20 19 18 17 16 15 14 13 12 11 10 9 8 7 6 5 4 3 2 1

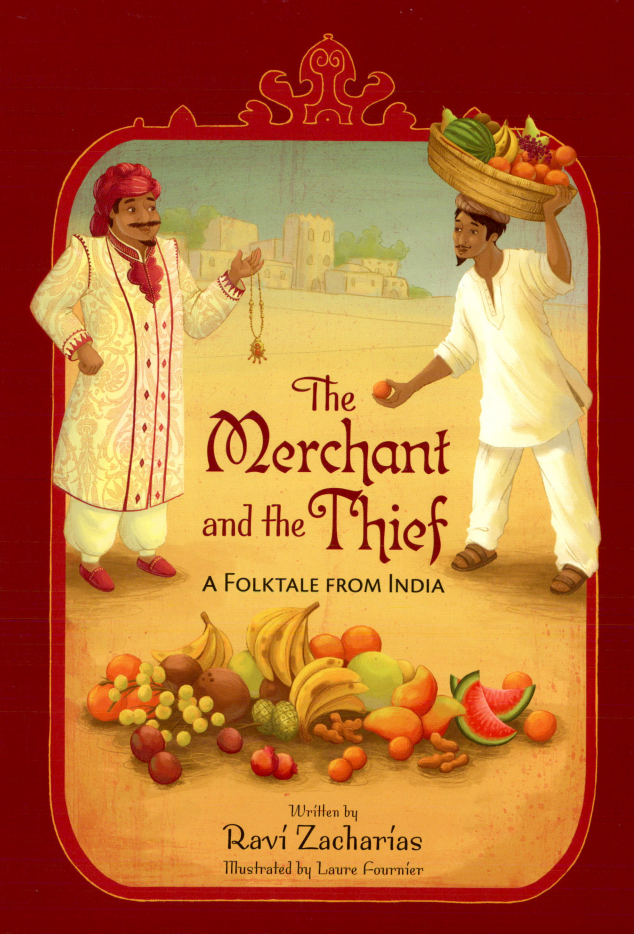

The Merchant and the Thief

A Folktale from India

Written by
Ravi Zacharias
Illustrated by Laure Fournier

ZONDERkidz

ZONDERVAN.com/
AUTHORTRACKER
follow your favorite authors

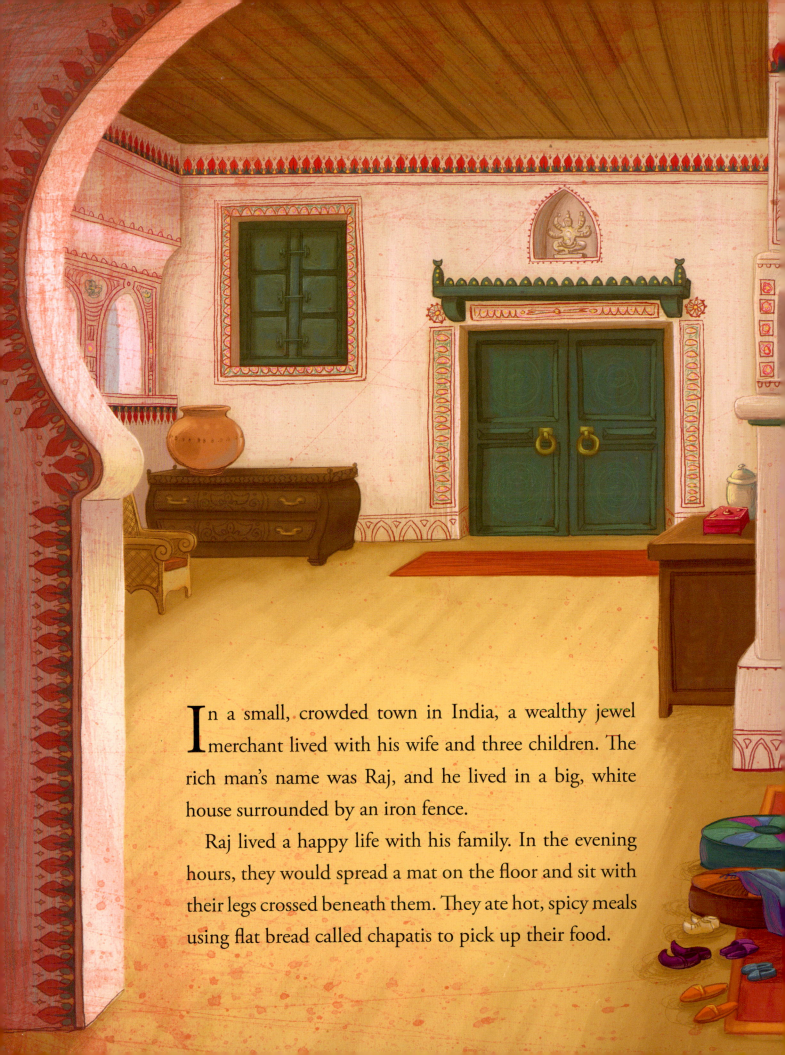

In a small, crowded town in India, a wealthy jewel merchant lived with his wife and three children. The rich man's name was Raj, and he lived in a big, white house surrounded by an iron fence.

Raj lived a happy life with his family. In the evening hours, they would spread a mat on the floor and sit with their legs crossed beneath them. They ate hot, spicy meals using flat bread called chapatis to pick up their food.

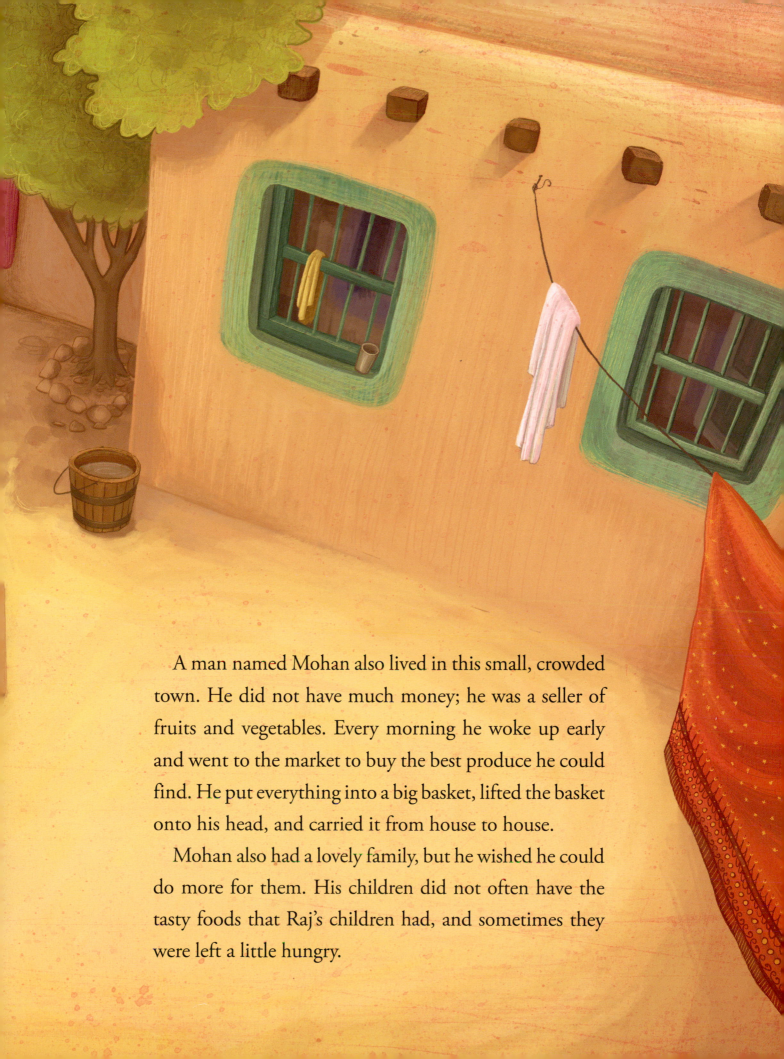

A man named Mohan also lived in this small, crowded town. He did not have much money; he was a seller of fruits and vegetables. Every morning he woke up early and went to the market to buy the best produce he could find. He put everything into a big basket, lifted the basket onto his head, and carried it from house to house.

Mohan also had a lovely family, but he wished he could do more for them. His children did not often have the tasty foods that Raj's children had, and sometimes they were left a little hungry.

Mohan began to think to himself, *I want to be rich like the people who live in big houses.* As he dreamed of all the things he wanted for his family, he began to steal little things. Sometimes he took extra vegetables from the market. Sometimes he did not give enough change to his customers.

Before he realized it, Mohan had become a thief.

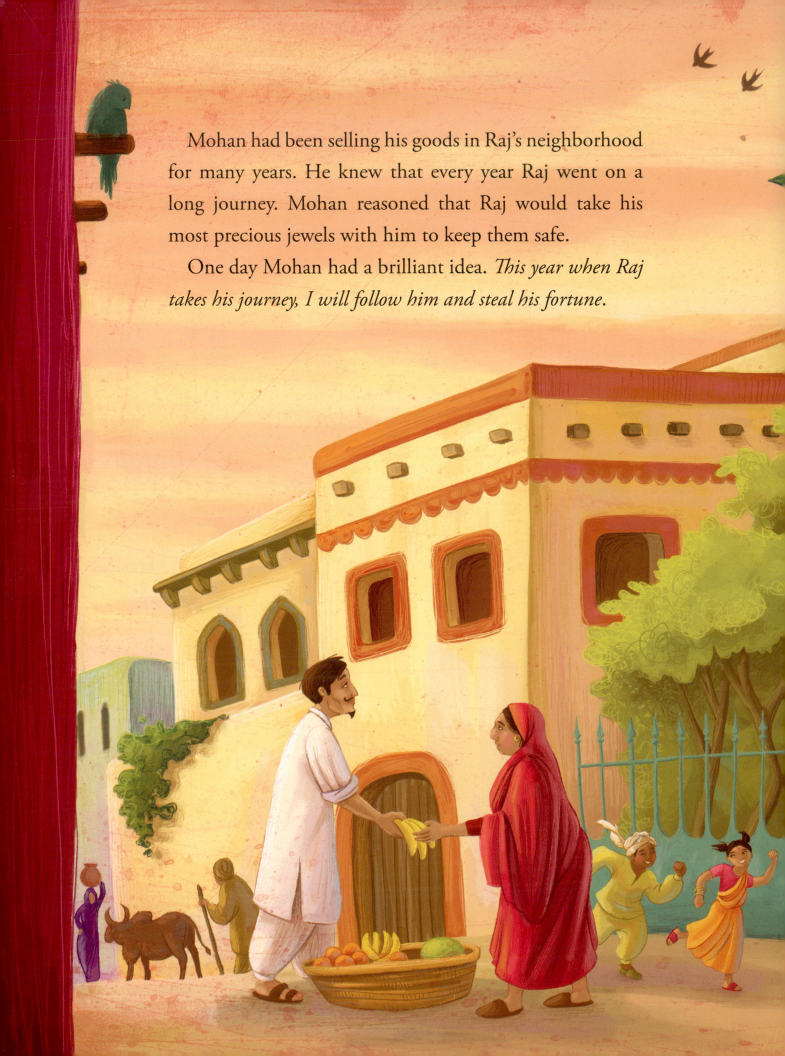

Mohan had been selling his goods in Raj's neighborhood for many years. He knew that every year Raj went on a long journey. Mohan reasoned that Raj would take his most precious jewels with him to keep them safe.

One day Mohan had a brilliant idea. *This year when Raj takes his journey, I will follow him and steal his fortune.*

On the day of his trip, Raj did indeed pack his most treasured jewels, including his mother's diamond wedding ring, a sapphire necklace for his daughter, and a gold bracelet he had chosen for his wife. There were many other precious pieces, as well as gifts for his sisters and brothers.

With his bag in one hand and a walking stick in the other, Raj said good-bye to his family. He set off at a steady pace, hoping to reach the next village by the end of the day.

Meanwhile, Mohan dressed in his best clothes so Raj would not guess how poor he really was. Mohan also kissed his family good-bye and then set out to follow Raj. Before long, Mohan was walking beside Raj and acting very friendly toward him.

At first Raj did not suspect that Mohan was planning to rob him, but he soon began to mistrust Mohan. Raj knew that the small roadside inns had few rooms and too many guests. Often two or more travelers had to share the same room, and he might be expected to share a room with Mohan. So Raj secretly made a plan to protect his treasure—and to teach Mohan an important lesson.

That evening they stopped at a little inn, and just as Raj expected, they were given a room to share. The innkeeper gave each of the men a mat and a pillow. He also gave each a towel, a basin, and soap to use before bed.

The men began to unpack their bags. Mohan had a plan. *I'll go out on the porch to wash my face. Then, when I return and Raj leaves the room, I'll find the jewels and run off into the night.*

But Raj had a plan of his own. While Mohan was outside, Raj hid his treasure in a place where he was sure the thief would never look.

When Raj went out onto the porch, Mohan raced to Raj's bag and searched frantically for the jewels. He dug his hands into the pockets of the bag and between the layers of clothing, but he could not find any treasure there. *I'll find those jewels tomorrow*, he thought angrily to himself, as Raj returned.

The next evening when the two men stopped, they shared a room again. When Mohan went out to the porch to clean up, Raj hid the jewels once more.

This time Mohan was certain he knew where the treasure was hidden. When Raj left the room, Mohan tiptoed over to Raj's belongings and searched hurriedly under his pillow. Again he found nothing. Now he was really upset.

The same thing happened each night. Mohan searched in Raj's bag, under his mat, and even in his coat pockets.

In the middle of the night, while Raj was sound asleep and snoring heavily, Mohan quietly slipped out of bed. He searched in the wastebasket and under every piece of furniture in the room. He wondered if he was mistaken about Raj having any treasure at all.

On the last afternoon of their journey, Raj looked into Mohan's eyes. "Mohan," he said, "I want to let you in on a little secret. I know you want my jewels. Although you thought you looked everywhere for them, there is one place you did not look. The treasure was under your own pillow all the time."

Mohan was shocked that every night he had laid his head on the treasure, yet he had never looked beneath his pillow.

"When we have our eyes on other people's treasure, we cannot see how close we are to the greatest treasure there is," Raj said. "Anyone can have this treasure, Mohan, even you."

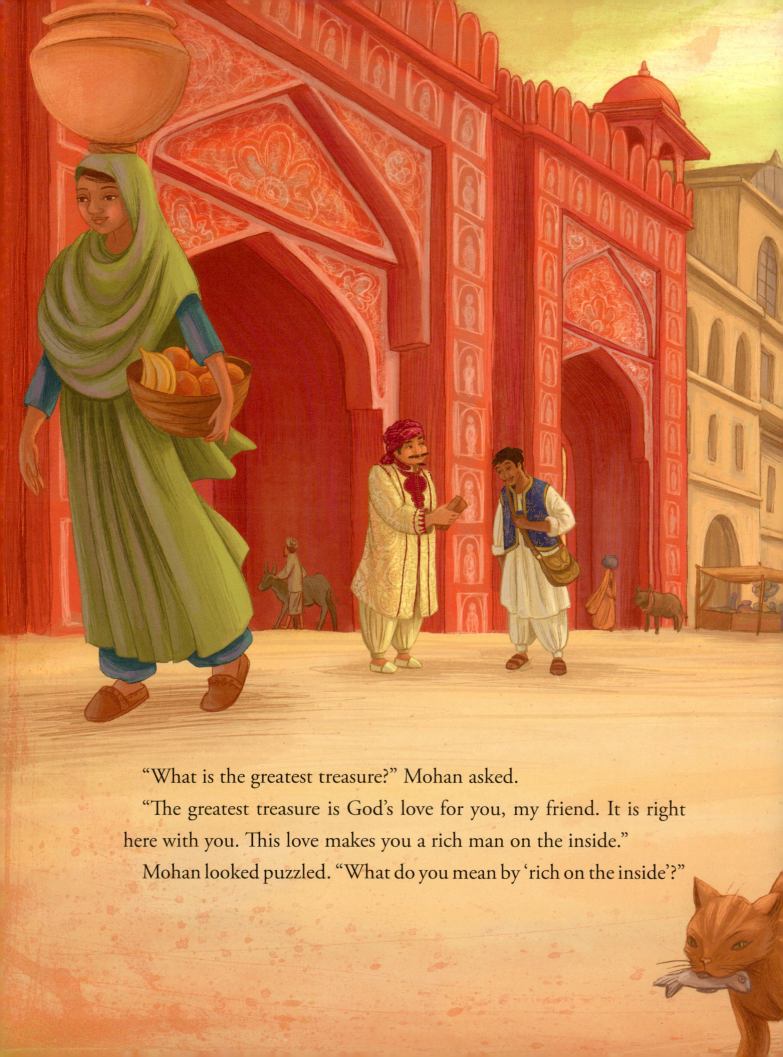

"What is the greatest treasure?" Mohan asked.

"The greatest treasure is God's love for you, my friend. It is right here with you. This love makes you a rich man on the inside."

Mohan looked puzzled. "What do you mean by 'rich on the inside'?"

Raj took out a small Bible and showed Mohan that God had given his best—the gift of his son Jesus Christ. Raj explained that when you give your life to Jesus, God makes you his own child. God loves his children and cares for their every need.

Feeling ashamed, Mohan knelt down and begged for Raj's forgiveness.

Raj helped Mohan to his feet. For the first time, Mohan stopped to think about what he had become. He thought of all God's blessings—his wife and children, his job, his friends. Those were things money could not buy.

"How good it is to know that God cares for me and my family," Mohan said. "I, too, want that treasure … God's love, in my heart."

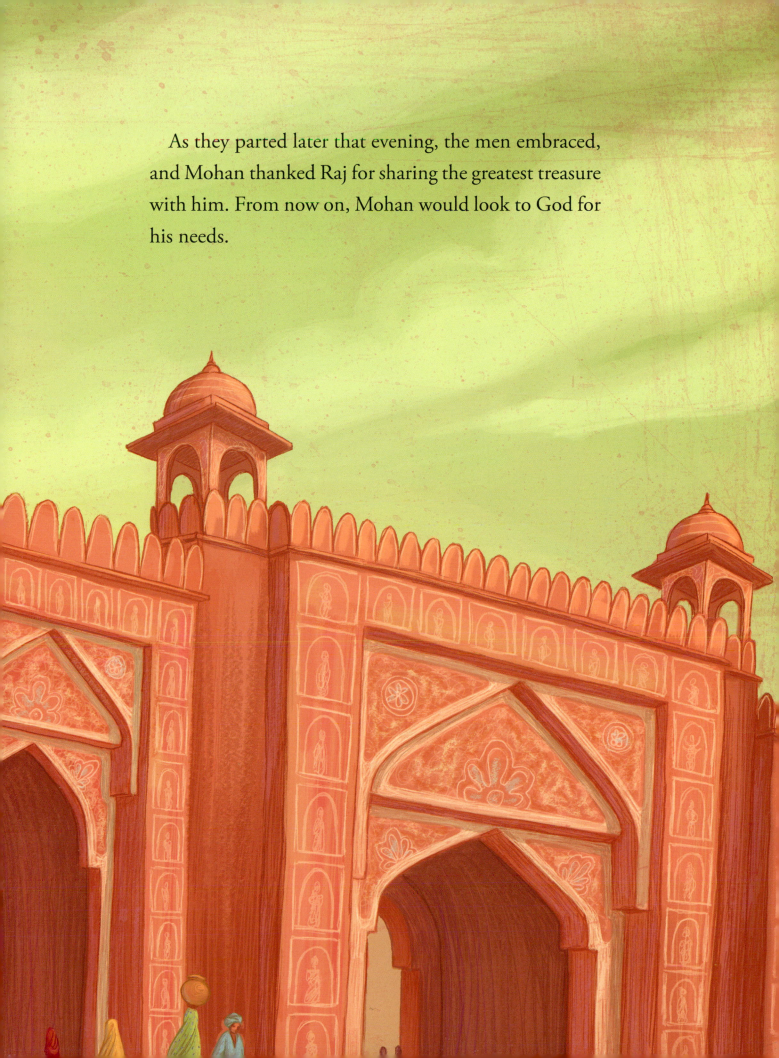

As they parted later that evening, the men embraced, and Mohan thanked Raj for sharing the greatest treasure with him. From now on, Mohan would look to God for his needs.

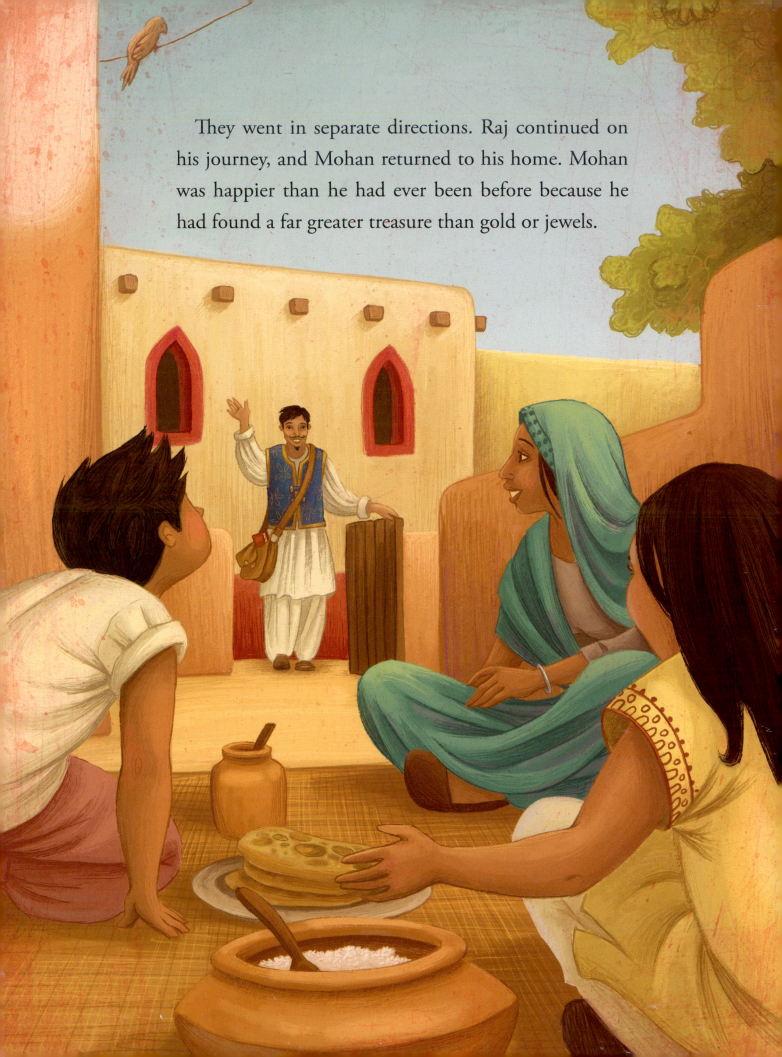

They went in separate directions. Raj continued on his journey, and Mohan returned to his home. Mohan was happier than he had ever been before because he had found a far greater treasure than gold or jewels.